THE CASSETTE LETTERS: A PSYCHOLOGICAL MYSTERY THRILLER BOOK OF FORGOTTEN MEMORIES AND DARK FAMILY SECRETS. (MISTERY, SUPENSE AND THRILLER BOOKS FOR ADULTS)

(PSYCHOLOGICAL MYSTERY BOOK 1) SHE INHERITED A BOX OF CASSETTE TAPES. WHAT SHE UNCOVERED WAS A PAST SHE WAS NEVER MEANT TO REMEMBER.

MARGOT SINCLAIR

CONTENTS

1. The Shoebox   1
2. Pressing Play   5
3. First Clues   9
4. The Silverwood Motel (New Mexico)   12
5. The Echo Studios Connection (Chicago)   16
6. A Ghost in Halcyon (Oregon)   21
7. A Hidden Name   26
8. A Warning From the Past   30
9. The Cabin in Montana   34
10. The Final Tape   38
11. Prologue - The Undeveloped Past   44

1

THE SHOEBOX

The funeral was smaller than Ellie expected.
A dozen or so mourners, most of them strangers. A few whispered condolences. A smattering of polite nods. But there was no real grief in the air, no raw sorrow clinging to the damp afternoon. Just the distant hum of rain and the practiced cadence of the priest's voice, reading words that felt as though they belonged to someone else's grandmother.

Ellie stood at the back, hands buried deep in the pockets of her black coat, shifting her weight from one foot to the other. She felt like an imposter, like someone who had wandered into a life she had only half-claimed.

Helen Mercer had been a woman of silence. A presence in Ellie's life, yes, but never a warmth. Never a guide. She had existed on the periphery, neither cruel nor kind, always just out of reach.

Ellie had met her a handful of times as a child—stiff, formal visits to a house that smelled of dust and mothballs, where the tea was always too bitter and the conversations too shallow. She had learned, early on, that her grandmother was not a woman of stories, not one for lullabies or laughter.

And now she was gone.

Ellie wasn't sure why she came. Obligation? Guilt? Some instinctive pull toward a family that had never truly felt like her own? Maybe, deep down, she had hoped that standing here, watching the casket sink into the earth, she might feel something real.

But she didn't.

The first handful of dirt hit the coffin with a soft thud. Then another. Then another.

It was over.

The rain began in a quiet drizzle at first, then heavier, pattering against the fabric of black umbrellas unfurling around her like inkblots against the gray sky. The small crowd dispersed quickly, vanishing into cars, into the mist. Ellie turned to leave, relieved that it was finally done—

Then she heard her name.

"Eleanor?"

She stopped.

The voice belonged to Richard Davenport, her grandmother's lawyer.

He was a tall man, late sixties, with a face carved by experience and suits that never wrinkled. He approached her with the practiced ease of someone who had spent a lifetime delivering quiet, measured news.

"I was hoping you'd stay for a moment." He pulled a small, worn **shoebox** from his briefcase. "Your grandmother left something for you."

Ellie frowned. **"For me?"**

Richard nodded. The box in his hands was **old**, the edges worn, the cardboard soft from age. A simple white sticker was pressed to the top, and in faded ink, her name was scrawled in neat, slanted cursive.

Ellie Mercer.

She hesitated before reaching for it.

The weight was unexpected—not heavy, but **solid**. Something inside shifted as she cradled it in her arms.

"She asked me to give this to you personally." Richard's voice softened, his usual professionalism thinning just a little at the edges. "Said you'd know when it was time."

Ellie studied the box. A strange, cold feeling stirred in her chest, something distant and unfamiliar.

Did she say anything else?

Richard hesitated. "Only that you'd understand when you listened."

Ellie's fingers curled slightly around the edges of the shoebox.

Listened.

She exhaled slowly, nodding. "Thanks."

Richard gave her a brief nod, as if considering whether to say more, then seemed to think better of it. Instead, he simply walked away, his shoes sinking slightly into the wet grass, leaving her alone in the rain with **a dead woman's secret in her hands.**

Back at the Apartment

The shoebox sat untouched for hours.

Ellie had placed it on the small wooden coffee table in her apartment, then proceeded to **ignore it**—walking past it again and again as she made tea she didn't drink, scrolled through her phone without reading a single word, paced from one side of her living room to the other, restless with something she couldn't quite name.

She wasn't sure **why** she hesitated.

It was just a box. **Just an object.**

But the moment Richard handed it to her, something inside her had shifted—like the air had become **thicker**, heavier, pressing down on her shoulders in a way she couldn't explain.

Eventually, the silence became unbearable.

She sat on the floor, cross-legged, and **pulled the shoebox into her lap.**

Her fingertips skimmed over the faded ink of her name before she took a deep breath and **pulled off the lid.**

Inside, neatly arranged, was a stack of **cassette tapes.**

Ellie's breath hitched.

The tapes were **old**, the labels yellowed and worn. Some were numbered in fading pen. Others had short, cryptic titles scrawled in her grandmother's slanted handwriting.

Halcyon.

Echo.

Silverwood.

But it was the **top tape** that made her pulse quicken.

There was no case, no protective sleeve. The label was handwritten, uneven from what looked like **a shaking hand.**

For You, When It's Time.

Ellie swallowed hard.

She turned the cassette over in her hands, her fingers tracing the edges.

The reels inside were still intact, the brown magnetic tape wound tightly. Waiting.

Waiting for what?

She didn't know.

But suddenly, for the first time in **years**, Ellie **wished she still had a cassette player.**

2

PRESSING PLAY

*E*llie didn't sleep that night.

The shoebox sat on the kitchen table like an open wound, its contents untouched since she first pulled off the lid. She had placed the cover back on, but it didn't matter. The weight of it wasn't in the cardboard or the plastic cassettes inside—it was in the air, thick and pressing, a silent presence lingering in the dim glow of her kitchen.

Her mother's voice was in there. **Waiting.**

For fifteen years, Margaret Mercer had been nothing more than a **distant memory**, a name signed on old birthday cards, a fading photograph tucked inside an old textbook Ellie hadn't opened in years. **Gone.** A slow, withering death in a hospice two states away, while Ellie was still in college.

They had never been particularly close. Margaret had loved in ways that were **difficult to hold onto**—like trying to catch mist in her fingers. There had been warmth, but it was fleeting, hidden behind sharp glances and closed doors. She had always been **distant, secretive**—a mother who carried her love like a locked box, offering glimpses but never giving it fully.

Ellie had never expected anything from her, especially not this.

A **message from beyond the grave.**

Her eyes flickered to the single tape she had set aside.
For You, When It's Time.

It sat beside her **half-empty coffee mug**, a relic from a past she hadn't known still existed. A puzzle piece she had no picture for.

She should have left it alone.

But Ellie had never been good at walking away.

The Search for a Player

By morning, she had made up her mind.

There was just one problem.

She didn't own a cassette player.

For all the weight this box carried, it was just **plastic and ribbon** without the right machine to make it speak. And so, she found herself pacing the aisles of a **dingy thrift shop on the outskirts of town**, the smell of old books and stale air pressing around her.

She sifted through a pile of electronics, ignoring broken CD players and cracked remote controls, until her fingers brushed something **small, rectangular, and yellow.**

A **Sony Walkman.**

It was scratched, the buttons worn down from years of use. The kind joggers had strapped to their belts in the '80s, the kind her mother might have once owned.

Ellie **turned it over in her hands**, pressing the eject button. The cassette door creaked open, empty.

This would do.

She grabbed a **pack of AA batteries** from the checkout and paid in cash, half-expecting the old man behind the counter to give her a **knowing look**, as if he somehow knew what she was about to do.

But he just took the money, shoved the Walkman in a paper bag, and went back to reading his newspaper.

Ellie walked out into the morning haze, the bag **heavier than it should have been** in her grip.

. . .

The Voice from the Past

Back at her apartment, she sat on the couch, staring at the Walkman on the coffee table.

She almost didn't press play.

Almost.

But hesitation had never been her strongest trait.

Ellie **popped the cassette into the player**, slid the worn headphones over her ears, and pressed the play button with a soft click.

The first sound was static.

A low, **hissing white noise**, like a radio struggling to find a station.

Then—**a voice.**

Her mother's voice.

"Ellie. If you're hearing this… then I know you've started looking."

Her breath caught in her throat.

It had been **so long** since she'd heard that voice.

And yet, it was **younger than she remembered**—not the tired, fading voice from the hospice bed. This was **before.** Long before.

Ellie swallowed hard.

"I don't know how much you know by now. Maybe nothing. Maybe everything. But if you're listening, I need you to promise me something."

A pause. A breath.

"Promise me you won't go too far."

A shiver **traced down Ellie's spine.**

What the hell did that mean?

She pressed the headphones **tighter** against her ears, barely breathing.

"There are things you don't remember. Things I tried to keep from you. Not because I wanted to lie… but because some truths don't belong to us."

"Some things are better left buried."

Buried.

The word settled in Ellie's chest like a cold stone.

She didn't move.

Didn't breathe.

The tape **crackled**, like it had been **partially recorded over.**

For a second, she thought it was over.

But then—

"There was a time before you, Ellie. A time before I was just your mother. And I need you to understand that everything started long before you were born."

Her fingers **tightened** around the Walkman.

She wanted to stop. **Fast forward. Rewind. Something—anything—to make this make sense.**

But the voice kept going.

"It started with a journey. And it started with A."

Ellie frowned.

A.

A person? A place?

Before she could think too hard about it, the **tape cut out.**

Silence.

Then—**abruptly, the recording resumed.**

But her mother's voice had **changed.**

Lower. More urgent.

"The tapes will show you the way. But be careful, Ellie."

"Some things once heard... can't be unheard."

Then—static.

The tape ended.

Ellie sat **frozen**, the Walkman still in her hands.

She **stared at the shoebox on the table**, at the **dozens of other tapes waiting inside.**

She had thought this was just **a relic of the past**.

A sentimental thing. A curiosity.

But it wasn't.

This was **a message. A warning.**

And it had only just begun.

3

FIRST CLUES

The room felt smaller.

The weight of the shoebox on the table was heavier now, as if it carried more than just old cassette tapes—**something buried, something dangerous.**

Ellie sat frozen, the last words of her mother's voice still echoing in her mind.

"Promise me you won't go too far."

But she was already past that point.

Her fingers hovered over the next tape in the stack. The label was **smudged**, ink faded from time, but she could still make out the name written across it.

Halcyon.

Ellie traced the letters, a strange, distant familiarity tickling the back of her mind.

A place? A person?

She didn't know. But **Margaret had left it for her for a reason.**

Ellie exhaled slowly and set the tape aside, her pulse steady but sharp. **She needed more.**

She reached back into the box, fingers pressing between the

cassettes, and felt something different—**thin, papery, delicate with age.**

She pulled it free and carefully unfolded it.

A **piece of paper**, yellowed at the edges, creased from being folded too many times. The ink had faded, but the words were still legible.

Silverwood Motel – New Mexico
Echo Studios – Chicago
Halcyon – Oregon

Ellie's stomach tightened.

These weren't just random words. **They were locations.**

A map. A trail her mother had left behind.

She could almost picture it—Margaret sitting somewhere, maybe at a desk, maybe at a kitchen table, writing these names down in her careful, slanted handwriting. **Planning.**

Ellie pressed her fingers to her temples, trying to make sense of it.

Why these places?

What connected them?

And why was her mother leading her **back** to them?

The Weight of the Past

Margaret had always been **a private person**, secretive even when she was alive. She spoke in half-truths, kept doors locked, left questions unanswered.

But this? **This was something else.**

This wasn't just secrecy.

This was **deliberate.**

A puzzle left behind.

A trail, waiting to be followed.

Ellie felt a dull ache press behind her ribs, **the weight of the unknown tightening around her.**

For fifteen years, she had kept her distance from Margaret's memory, refusing to let herself get tangled in the past. She told herself she was **better off not knowing** the answers.

But that was a lie.

She had **always wanted to know.**

And now, Margaret was giving her a chance.

Ellie looked at the **Walkman**, the tape still waiting inside.

The other cassettes held answers—she **knew** that now.

But sitting here, listening to old recordings, wouldn't be enough.

A Decision That Can't Be Undone

She glanced back at the **note**, her pulse steady but tight.

New Mexico.

Chicago.

Oregon.

She had to go.

Had to see it for herself.

Had to **trace Margaret's footsteps, step into the echoes of her past, and find out what the hell her mother had been trying to tell her.**

Her grip **tightened** around the note.

She had promised herself she wouldn't fall into the past.

Wouldn't let herself **chase ghosts.**

Wouldn't let herself get **lost in something she couldn't fix.**

But it was too late for that now.

Because this wasn't just about Margaret.

It was about **something bigger.**

Something that had been waiting for her to find it.

And she was done waiting.

4

THE SILVERWOOD MOTEL (NEW MEXICO)

The **Silverwood Motel** sat on the edge of the desert, a relic from another time, as if the world had moved forward but left it behind.

The neon sign **buzzed weakly**, its pink glow flickering in and out, half the letters missing so that it barely spelled **SILV—WOOD MOT** — against the backdrop of the vast, empty sky. The building itself was tired—**faded stucco walls, sun-bleached doors, a cracked swimming pool filled with dust instead of water.** A place where time had stopped, but ghosts had lingered.

Ellie pulled into the nearly deserted parking lot, killing the engine.

For a long moment, she didn't move.

Her hands clenched around the steering wheel, her knuckles white. She had driven almost **ten hours** to get here, guided only by a **list of names and places** scribbled on a **faded piece of paper**—a breadcrumb trail her mother had left behind.

And now, **staring at this forgotten motel in the middle of nowhere**, she couldn't shake the feeling that she had made a mistake.

She reached for the **shoebox on the passenger seat**, tracing her fingers over the cassette tapes inside.

"**This is where it started,**" her mother's voice had said.

So this was where she had to begin.

With a deep breath, Ellie grabbed her bag, stepped out into the **warm desert air**, and walked toward the motel office.

A Name from the Past

The **office smelled of stale coffee and nicotine**, the ceiling fan creaking overhead as it pushed thick, unmoving air around the small room. Behind the counter, a woman sat, her **hair piled into a messy bun**, a cigarette dangling lazily between her fingers.

She looked up as Ellie entered, her eyes **sharp despite the haze of smoke curling around her.**

Ellie pulled a **photograph of Margaret** from her pocket and slid it across the counter.

"**Do you remember her?**"

The woman squinted at the photo, tapping her cigarette against the ashtray before picking it up for a closer look.

Her lips parted slightly, something flickering across her expression.

"Margaret... yeah, I remember her." She exhaled slowly. "**She stayed here for a few months. Back in '87, I think.**"

Ellie's **pulse quickened.**

"**Did she say why she was here?**"

Gloria—her name was embroidered in faded red thread on her shirt—gave Ellie a slow, measured look.

"**She was pregnant.**"

Ellie's breath **hitched.**

Pregnant.

That **didn't make sense.**

Ellie was born in **1989.**

If Margaret had been pregnant in '**87**, that meant—

There had been another child.

A sibling.

The realization settled like a stone in Ellie's stomach, heavy and cold.

"Do you know what happened to the baby?" she asked, forcing the words out.

Gloria shook her head. "**She left one night. No warning. Didn't even check out. Just... gone.**"

Ellie's hands **curled into fists.**

Margaret had run.

But from **what?**

Or from **who?**

Gloria flicked her cigarette into the ashtray and leaned on the counter. "**If you're looking for answers, she stayed in Room 6. Still rent it out. Nothing's changed much.**"

Ellie **nodded. "I'll take it."**

Room 6

The room smelled of **old carpet and cigarette smoke**, the walls tinged yellow with age.

A **dull floral bedspread** stretched over the mattress, faded with time. The **nightstand was missing a drawer**, and the TV remote sat abandoned on top of it, covered in a thin layer of dust.

Ellie **stood in the doorway**, her bag slipping from her shoulder.

She tried to **picture her mother here**, nearly two years before Ellie was born, carrying **another child**—a sibling she had never known existed.

She **ran her fingers over the walls**, the furniture, as if touching the past might make it real.

Her gaze drifted downward.

The carpet near the bed was **slightly raised**, uneven against the floorboards.

She frowned, stepping closer. **Something was underneath.**

Kneeling, she **peeled back the fabric**, her hands **tugging at the edges until it pulled free.** The wood beneath was rough, but there— just beneath the boards—she saw it.

A **cassette tape.**

It had been **hidden for decades**, the label **faded** but still legible.

SILVERWOOD. 1987.

Ellie's heart pounded.

She slid the tape into her **Walkman**, pressed the **headphones over her ears**, and hit **play**.

Static.

Then—**her mother's voice.**

"This is where it started. This is where I made my choice."

The tape crackled.

Ellie **held her breath.**

Then, in a voice **barely above a whisper—**

"If you've found this, then you're closer than you should be."

The tape **cut off.**

Silence.

Ellie's **blood ran cold.**

Her mother's voice had been **low, urgent, almost afraid.**

She wasn't just following a trail.

She was **walking into something Margaret had tried to leave behind.**

And someone, somewhere, **might not want her to find the rest.**

5

THE ECHO STUDIOS CONNECTION (CHICAGO)

The **Echo Studios building** was a ghost of itself.

Ellie stood on the cracked sidewalk, staring up at the faded marquee sign, its letters barely legible through layers of grime:

ECHO STUDIOS – RECORDING & PRODUCTION

The sign flickered once, then died again. **As if it had tried to remember something long forgotten.**

The **windows were dark**, streaked with dust and rain stains. A **rusted chain wrapped tightly around the front doors**, secured by a heavy padlock. A **condemned notice** was taped to the glass, its edges curled with age.

Ellie **checked the address again**, but there was no mistake.

This was the place.

Her mother had been here.

And for the first time since she had started following Margaret's trail, **Ellie felt the weight of what she was doing settle deep in her bones.**

This wasn't just a list of locations anymore.

This wasn't just a mystery to unravel.

She was stepping into the past her mother had abandoned.

And something told her she wouldn't like what she found.

. . .

Inside the Studio

Ellie expected to have to break in.

She didn't.

Someone already had.

The **side door hung slightly open**, its **lock shattered**, as if someone had forced their way in long before she arrived.

She hesitated.

Her heartbeat **quickened**.

Something about the way the door hung open—**not wide enough for an invitation, but just enough to suggest someone had been here recently**—made her pulse pound against her ribs.

Still, she stepped forward.

The door **groaned on its hinges** as she nudged it open.

The air inside was **thick with dust**, the scent of old wood and rusting metal clinging to the silence.

The hallway leading deeper into the studio was lined with **old, peeling recording posters**, their edges curling from age. Some she recognized—**big names from the '80s**—but most had faded into obscurity, their images distorted by time.

At the end of the hall, the main recording studio **sat abandoned**.

A grand piano, untouched and out of tune.

A mixing console covered in dust.

A broken microphone stand leaning in the corner like an exhausted ghost.

And in the corner—**a stack of old demo tapes.**

Ellie's fingers hovered over the reels.

Most of the labels were nothing special—**band names, track lists, scribbled song titles.**

But one stood out.

Margaret M. – Private Session.

Ellie's **stomach flipped**.

She reached for it—

Then a **voice behind her made her freeze.**

. . .

A Name from the Past

"That's a name I haven't heard in a long time."

Ellie **spun around, pulse hammering.**

An **older man stood in the doorway**, his gray hair tucked beneath a worn baseball cap. His **clothes were covered in paint stains**, like he had been working on something before wandering in.

His **eyes swept over the room**, then landed on the cassette still clutched in Ellie's fingers.

"**You knew my mother?**" Ellie asked, tightening her grip on the tape.

The man studied her, **his expression unreadable.**

"Margaret Mercer?" He nodded slowly. "**Yeah. I knew her.**"

Ellie took a slow breath. "**I need to know why she was here.**"

The man hesitated, then motioned toward a **dusty chair in the corner.**

"**She was recording.**" He exhaled. "**But it wasn't just music.**"

Who Was Daniel Calloway?

His name was **Victor Reyes**.

A retired **session guitarist** who had once worked at **Echo Studios**.

"**Margaret was involved with someone here,**" Victor said, rubbing his chin. "**A producer. Daniel Calloway.**"

Ellie felt the name like a **pulse in her chest.**

Calloway.

It was **familiar—too familiar.**

She had seen it before.

Astrid Calloway.

The name on the **birth certificate she found in Montana.**

The first child.

Ellie's breath hitched. "**Who was Daniel Calloway?**"

Victor **sighed**, like the answer carried its own weight.

"**Brilliant, but reckless.**" He shook his head. "**Always pushing limits. Experimenting with sound. With memory.**"

Ellie frowned. "**Memory?**"

Victor hesitated. "**You wouldn't believe me if I told you.**"

Ellie's pulse pounded. "**Try me.**"

Victor exhaled. "**He left suddenly. No warning. Right around the same time Margaret did.**"

Ellie swallowed hard. "**When?**"

Victor's eyes **darkened**.

"**Back in '87.**"

The Hidden Tape

Ellie's mind was **spinning**.

Margaret had **disappeared the same time as Calloway.**

The **same year she had been pregnant.**

None of this was **coincidence.**

She turned back to the **cassette still clenched in her hand.**

Victor's gaze followed hers.

"That was her last session," he said quietly.

Ellie hesitated.

Then, slowly, she slid the tape into her **Walkman**.

The hiss of static filled her ears.

Then—**Margaret's voice.**

"**I don't have much time. If you're listening to this, then you know by now. About the baby. About Astrid.**"

Ellie's **breath caught.**

"**I tried to keep her safe. I did everything I could. But I wasn't the only one looking for her.**"

Looking for her?

Ellie pressed the headphones tighter, but the tape **crackled—distorted, skipping like someone had erased pieces of it.**

Then Margaret's voice returned, **urgent now.**

"**Don't trust Calloway. He—**"

Silence.

The tape **cut out.**

Ellie **yanked the headphones off**, her pulse **hammering** in her ears.

Calloway.

Her mother had **warned her about him.**

But why?

And more importantly—**was he still out there?**

Ellie looked down at the **Walkman in her hands.**

The tape had **stopped.**

But she wasn't done listening.

Not yet.

She turned back to Victor.

"**What was he experimenting with?**"

Victor hesitated.

Then, quietly, he said:

"**Not just music.**"

"**Memories.**"

6

A GHOST IN HALCYON (OREGON)

*E*llie **drove into Halcyon just before sunset**, the sky painted in soft oranges and fading pinks.

It wasn't much of a town—just a handful of **weathered buildings**, a **single gas station**, and a **diner with a flickering neon sign** struggling to stay lit. A place that felt **forgotten**, untouched by time, where the world outside had moved forward, but Halcyon had remained exactly as it was.

Ellie slowed the car, her fingers **tight on the wheel** as she scanned the near-empty streets.

If Margaret had lived here—even briefly—**someone had to remember her.**

She wasn't expecting to find **ghosts.**

Not yet.

The Woman Who Remembered

The **diner smelled like old grease and burnt coffee**, the kind of scent that never really faded no matter how many times the place was cleaned. A few **old men sat at the counter**, their conversations slow, voices gravelly from years of cigarettes and whiskey.

They were talking about the **logging industry like it was still thriving.**

Ellie stepped inside, the **bell above the door jingling softly.**

A woman—**sixties, silver hair pulled back into a tight bun**—stood behind the counter, wiping down the **already-clean** surface with a practiced motion.

Ellie approached, pulling the **photograph of Margaret** from her pocket and sliding it onto the counter.

"**Excuse me**," she said, her voice steady. "**Do you recognize her?**"

The woman stilled.

Her **face changed immediately.**

Ellie saw it in her **eyes first**—the flicker of recognition, the hesitation, the way her grip on the dishrag **tightened just slightly.**

She knew.

"**Where did you get this?**" the woman asked, her voice tighter than before.

Ellie **kept her gaze steady.**

"**She was my mother.**" She chose her next words carefully. "**She stayed here in the late '80s. I'm trying to find out why.**"

The woman's **gaze flickered toward the door.**

Like she was checking to see if someone else was listening.

Like she had **something to say but didn't want to say it here.**

Then, finally—**a pause.**

And the words that sent a **cold wave through Ellie's chest.**

"Your mother... she had a baby with her."

A B**ABY** in Halcyon

Ellie's **stomach dropped.**

She leaned in. "**Are you sure?**"

The woman **nodded slowly.**

"I saw her. I remember because I never saw her again after that."

Ellie's fingers **tightened around the edge of the counter.**

She had expected **clues, vague hints, dead ends.**

But not this.
Not **confirmation**.
Not something that made it **impossible to ignore the truth anymore.**

Astrid wasn't just some name on a birth certificate.
She was real.

Ellie's breath was **unsteady** as she forced herself to ask, "What happened?"

The woman **hesitated**.

Like she didn't want to say.

Like she had **kept this story locked away for decades and wasn't sure if it was safe to bring it back out.**

Then, finally—**softly**.

"One night, she left. Just... disappeared."

Ellie's **pulse pounded**.

Just like in New Mexico.

Just like in Chicago.

Margaret had been **running**.

Again.

But from what?

Or from who?

The woman wiped her hands on the rag, then folded it over like she was done talking.

Ellie wanted to push.

She wanted **more**.

But there was something in the woman's **eyes now**—something **closed off, guarded.**

She wasn't going to say **anything else.**

The Man in the Dark

Ellie stepped outside, her **mind racing**.

A **baby**.

Margaret had **a baby with her in Halcyon**.

That meant **Astrid had been here**.

That meant **Margaret hadn't just given her up.**

She had **taken her somewhere. Hidden her.**

Ellie reached for her phone, ready to take notes, when she felt **it.**

A presence.

She lifted her gaze—

And **froze.**

Across the street, **leaning against a truck near the gas station**, stood a **man.**

Tall, wiry, dressed in an **old denim jacket** and a **baseball cap pulled low over his face.**

Watching her.

He wasn't **moving.**

He wasn't **pretending.**

It was **deliberate.**

Ellie's **heart pounded.**

The second she met his gaze—**he turned away.**

Then, **without a word**, he pushed off the truck and **walked toward the woods** at the edge of town.

Ellie's stomach tightened.

This wasn't **a coincidence.**

This wasn't **some local curious about the newcomer.**

She had **stirred something up.**

And **someone didn't want her asking questions.**

The Warning

Ellie **followed him.**

Only a few steps.

Just enough to see if he would turn around.

He didn't.

He **kept walking**, disappearing deeper into the **tree line**.

Then—**he stopped.**

Still facing away from her.

And **spoke.**

"Some questions don't need answers."

His **voice was low.**
Almost **casual.**
Ellie **froze.**
"**What does that mean?**" she asked, pulse hammering.
The man **exhaled**, shaking his head slightly.
"**It means you should leave before you find something you can't walk away from.**"
Cold fear slithered down Ellie's spine.
"**Did you know my mother?**" she asked, stepping forward.
The man **didn't answer.**
He just **turned and disappeared into the woods.**
Ellie **stood there**, heart **pounding** against her ribs.
A **threat.**
A **warning.**
Or **both.**
But one thing was **clear—**
She was getting too close.
To something that had been buried for over thirty years.
And someone, somewhere, didn't want it uncovered.

7

A HIDDEN NAME

The **motel room** was dimly lit, the glow from the bedside lamp **casting long shadows** against the peeling wallpaper.

Ellie sat **cross-legged on the bed**, the Walkman in her lap, fingers gripping the sides like it might slip through her grasp.

The **tape from Halcyon** was old, the edges of the cassette brittle, the reels inside struggling against time. The **audio was warped**, crackling under layers of **static and age**, but beneath it—**her mother's voice still lived.**

Ellie **closed her eyes**, pressing the headphones tighter against her ears, blocking out everything except the sound of the past whispering through the tape.

Margaret's voice came in fragments.

"...I had to leave... It wasn't safe..."

Ellie's breath **shallowed**.

"...I didn't have a choice..."

Then—**a name.**

Clear. Unmistakable.

"**Astrid.**"

Ellie's **lungs tightened**.

Astrid.

The name from the **birth certificate in Montana.**
The **baby** her mother had in **Halcyon.**
A **sibling Ellie never knew existed.**

The tape **warped again,** the distortion **swallowing Margaret's voice,** but Ellie caught another **faint whisper** just before the static surged—

"...I tried to keep her safe... but I wasn't the only one looking for her."

A chill **traced down Ellie's spine.**
Not **watching her.**
Not **finding her.**
Looking.
Who?
And why?

The tape **skipped violently,** static **overwhelming** whatever came next.

Ellie **ripped off the headphones,** her **pulse hammering** against her ribs.

She needed **more than just tapes.**
She needed **something solid.**

A **document.** Proof that Astrid wasn't just **a name whispered on an old cassette.**

And she had **one place left to check.**

The Birth Certificate

The **Halcyon town records office** was housed in a **squat brick building,** tucked between the **post office** and an **empty storefront with a 'For Lease' sign curling in the window.**

Inside, the air was **stale, thick with the scent of dust and old paper,** the kind of place where time didn't pass so much as **settle into the walls.**

Ellie approached the counter, her fingers **tight around the birth records request she had filled out.**

The clerk—a **woman in her seventies,** thick glasses perched on the end of her nose—barely **glanced up** as Ellie **slid the request across the counter.**

"I'm looking for anything under Margaret Mercer," Ellie said, **steadying her voice.** "From the late '80s."

The woman **studied her.**

Not **suspicious.**

Just... **curious.**

Then she shuffled off into the back **without a word.**

Ellie **exhaled slowly**, shifting her weight from foot to foot.

Five minutes passed.

Then ten.

Her **fingers tapped restlessly against the counter**, her mind spinning with the weight of **what she might find.**

Then—**finally.**

The clerk **reappeared.**

And she wasn't **holding one document.**

She was **holding two.**

Two Birth Certificates

Ellie's **hands trembled** as she reached for them.

The first one **was hers.**

Eleanor Margaret Mercer

Born: **July 3, 1989**

Mother: **Margaret Mercer**

Father: **Unknown**

Nothing surprising.

Nothing out of place.

Her entire **existence**, condensed into **a single sheet of paper.**

But the second—

Ellie's **stomach dropped.**

Astrid Calloway

Born: **1987**

Mother: **Margaret Mercer**

Father: **Daniel Calloway**

Ellie's **vision blurred** for a second as she **gripped the paper tighter.**

Calloway.

The man from Echo Studios.

The one **her mother had warned her about.**

The one who had **vanished the same time Margaret did.**

Ellie forced herself to **take a breath**, her heartbeat **loud in her ears.**

Her mother had said she tried to **keep Astrid safe.**

But from what? From who?

Ellie's **fingers curled** around the birth certificate.

She **hadn't imagined it.**

She **wasn't wrong.**

Someone had tried to **erase this.**

Someone had tried to **make Astrid disappear.**

But the records **were still here.**

And now—**Ellie had them.**

Her sister **existed.**

Which meant **one terrifying, inescapable truth.**

If she existed—then what happened to her?

8

A WARNING FROM THE PAST

The **motel room was silent**, save for the rhythmic hum of the air conditioner struggling against the heat.

Ellie sat hunched over the table, her elbows pressed into the worn wood, staring down at the two **birth certificates** spread out in front of her like puzzle pieces that didn't fit.

Her name.
Eleanor Margaret Mercer.
Born: **July 3, 1989.**
Astrid's name.
Astrid Calloway.
Born: **1987.**
Two daughters. **Two timelines.**
But something was wrong.

The photograph she had found in Halcyon **complicated everything**.

Margaret, holding a baby.
The date scrawled on the back? 1988.
A year after Astrid was supposedly born.
A year before Ellie was born.

Ellie's **stomach tightened** as the thought formed, unspoken and horrifying.

Who was in the picture?

Astrid?

Or Ellie?

And if the **timeline didn't match—**

Had there really been **two children?**

Or just **one child… twice?**

Ellie pressed a **hand to her temple**, her pulse drumming beneath her skin.

Her whole life, she had been one person.

Now, she wasn't sure if she had ever really belonged to herself.

She turned to the **shoebox of cassette tapes**.

Her mother had told her everything.

She just **hadn't been listening.**

Replaying the Past

Ellie shuffled through the **stack of tapes**, her fingers brushing against the worn labels.

Her mother's voice had given her **pieces** of the story—**cryptic fragments, warnings, whispers through time.**

But now that Ellie **knew the name Astrid**, she had to wonder…

Had Margaret already **told her the truth**—and she just hadn't understood it?

Her fingers found **one of the earlier tapes.**

The one she had **dismissed before.**

She **pressed play.**

"…Some things aren't meant to be remembered."

Ellie's **breath hitched.**

"…Not everything belongs to you."

Her **stomach knotted.**

She had heard that before—**Margaret repeating that phrase across different tapes.**

But now, with the **birth certificates in front of her**, the meaning **shifted.**

Not everything belongs to you.

What was Margaret saying?

That she **didn't belong to herself?**

Or worse—**that Ellie didn't belong to herself?**

A **shiver crawled down her spine.**

Ellie **grabbed another tape. Pressed play.**

"...I tried to fix it. I tried to keep it from happening again."

Happening again?

Ellie's **heartbeat thundered in her ears.**

"But it never really stops, does it? It just keeps repeating."

Ellie **ripped the headphones off,** her breath **shallow.**

Repeating.

Was that what this was?

Was **Astrid not just a missing sister... but another version of herself?**

The thought **made her dizzy.**

She **stared at the birth certificates again,** the dates **warping in her mind.**

If Margaret had **lost Astrid—**

And then had **Ellie—**

Had Ellie been **meant to replace someone?**

Or was she **someone who had already existed before?**

She **staggered away from the table,** her vision **blurring at the edges.**

This wasn't just about a **lost child.**

This was about a **loop.**

Something happening **over and over again.**

And Margaret had **tried to stop it.**

The Photo That Shouldn't Exist

Ellie needed **air.**

She grabbed her **bag**, stuffing the **tapes and birth certificates inside**, and stepped outside the **motel door**.

The sun was **setting over Halcyon**, casting the town in a **golden haze**, the light stretching **long shadows** across the empty streets.

She walked toward her car, her mind still racing, the fragments of her mother's voice **looping in her head**.

Then—

She **froze**.

A **manila envelope** was tucked under her **windshield wiper**.

Ellie's **pulse spiked**.

Her eyes **darted across the street**—searching.

But there was **no one**.

The town was **quiet**, too quiet, like it was **holding its breath**.

With **shaking hands**, she pulled the envelope free and **tore it open**.

Inside was **a single Polaroid**.

Ellie's **stomach twisted**.

It was her **mother**.

Standing in front of a cabin.

Holding a baby.

The **same photo from Halcyon**.

But this time—

There was something **new**.

A handwritten message, **scrawled across the bottom**.

"**Montana.**"

Ellie's **chest tightened**.

Someone had left this for her.

Someone **was watching**.

And they **wanted her to keep going**.

To **Montana**.

To the **cabin**.

To whatever came **next**.

9

THE CABIN IN MONTANA

The **road stretched endlessly ahead**, cutting through a vast expanse of **pine forests and frozen valleys**, a world untouched by time.

Montana was **quiet**, its silence deeper than anything Ellie had known. **Cold air curled through the trees**, shifting through the branches like whispers, like something unseen was moving alongside her. The sky above was so **wide and endless** that it felt like it could swallow her whole.

Ellie had been driving for hours, following the **handwritten message** scrawled on the bottom of the **Polaroid**.

Montana.

And now, as she turned onto a **narrow dirt road**, one that barely **existed on the map**, her pulse **thrummed in her ears.**

Because she **knew this place.**

Not from memory.

But from **somewhere deeper.**

Like a **dream she had never remembered until now.**

The Cabin

The **cabin** sat at the end of the road, tucked into the trees like it had been placed there and then **forgotten**.

It was **small, weathered**, its wooden planks **cracked with time**, its roof sagging under years of snow and rain. The **windows were dark**, black rectangles staring out into the woods, and the **front door hung slightly open.**

Ellie killed the engine.

She gripped the **steering wheel, her knuckles white.**

Something waited inside.

She could **feel it.**

She forced herself to move.

The cabin smelled of **dust, woodsmoke, and something older—something forgotten.**

It wasn't much inside.

- **A rickety bed**, the sheets moth-eaten and discolored.
- **A rusted stove**, long abandoned.
- **A table covered in old papers**, their edges curled and yellowed.

And in the corner—

Ellie's **breath caught.**

A **stack of drawings.**

Child's drawings.

The Drawings

Ellie **stepped closer**, her fingers **brushing the crumbling edges of the paper.**

There were **three drawings.**

The first—**a woman holding a baby.**

Ellie's **chest tightened.**

Her mother. Margaret.

The second—a **man with no face.**

Ellie's stomach twisted. The lines were **harsh, uneven**, like whoever had drawn it had been **afraid of what they were remembering.**

And the third—
Ellie's **pulse stopped.**
Two little girls.
One had **Ellie's name scrawled beneath it.**
The other—
Astrid.
Her **hands shook** as she **backed away.**
Her mother had **been here.**
Astrid had **been here.**
But had they been here **together?**
Or had they been here **at different times?**
The thought sent a shiver **through Ellie's bones.**
She wasn't sure which answer was **worse.**

The Last Tape

The fireplace was **cold**, its hearth covered in **a thin layer of soot** and ash.
Something **glinted beneath the dust.**
Ellie **knelt**, brushing away the debris with **shaking hands.**
A **rusted film canister.**
Something **rattled inside.**
She pried the **lid off.**
And there it was.
The **last cassette tape.**
Ellie's **fingers were numb** as she placed it into the **Walkman.**
She pressed **play.**
Static.
Then—**Margaret's voice.**
Tired. Broken. Afraid.
"Ellie... **If you've come this far, you already know the truth.**"
Ellie's **breath hitched.**
"**I had two daughters.**"
Her heart **pounded.**
"**One was taken. One was left behind.**"

Ellie's **skin went cold.**
"And one of you... doesn't belong."
The words **sent ice through her veins.**
One of you doesn't belong.
The tape **crackled**, the static swelling, as if something **had been erased.**
Ellie's **pulse thundered in her ears.**
What did that mean?
Which one of them **wasn't supposed to exist?**

The **Footsteps**

Then—**a sound outside.**
Ellie went still.
A **footstep on dead leaves.**
Another.
Close.
Ellie **ripped the headphones off,** her heart **slamming against her ribs.**
The **front door creaked.**
A **shadow passed over the window.**
Ellie **grabbed the tape, the canister, anything she could,** and stepped back into the **darkness of the cabin.**
The **floor groaned beneath her weight.**
She **held her breath.**
She wasn't alone.
Someone had **been waiting for her.**
Someone had **followed her here.**
And as the **door slowly creaked open,** Ellie realized—
This wasn't just about **the past anymore.**
The past had found her.
And it **wasn't finished yet.**

10

THE FINAL TAPE

The **door creaked open.**
Ellie's breath **caught in her throat**, her body frozen between the past whispering in her ears and the presence standing just beyond the threshold.

The air in the **cabin had been thick with dust and time**, but now it felt suffocating—**alive with something unseen.**

A **shadow filled the doorway.**

Neither of them moved.

Ellie gripped the **Walkman**, the final tape still playing, her mother's voice murmuring in the background—**but she barely heard it.**

The only thing she could hear was **her own heartbeat, erratic and deafening in her ears.**

Then—**a step forward.**

The **floorboards groaned** beneath the figure's weight.

A second step.

Ellie's **instincts took over.**

She **darted backward**, knocking over a **rusted chair**, her body **slamming against the table** as she scrambled to **find something—anything—to defend herself.**

Her pulse **pounded** as she reached for **the only weapon in sight—** a **broken fireplace poker** resting against the stone hearth.

She gripped it **tight**, her knuckles white.

"Who are you?" she demanded, her voice **sharper than she expected, desperate and raw.**

No answer.

The shadow **moved closer.**

And then, as the dim light from the oil lamp flickered over the figure's face—

Ellie **stopped breathing.**

Because she wasn't staring at a **stranger.**

She was staring at **herself.**

THE OTHER ELLIE

Ellie felt the ground **tilt beneath her.**

Her hands **trembled against the cold iron of the poker**, her breath coming in short, ragged gasps.

No. No, no, no.

The **Other Ellie** stepped forward, moving like she belonged here— **like this was her cabin, her space.**

She wasn't **identical.**

This **Ellie**—the one standing in front of her—was **thinner, paler, her hair slightly longer, tangled at the edges like she had been walking through the woods for years.**

Her **clothes were faded, dusted with dirt**, her bare arms **bruised and scratched**, as if she had been **clawing through time itself.**

But it was her.

Ellie's stomach twisted into a knot so tight she thought she might be sick.

"**This isn't real,**" she whispered, more to herself than to the figure. "**You're not real.**"

The **Other Ellie cocked her head** slightly—the **exact way Ellie did when she was thinking.**

A perfect mirror.
Then, finally, she spoke.
"That's what I thought about you."
Ellie's **vision swam.**
Her grip **loosened** on the poker.
She felt her **heartbeat slow, like her body was trying to reject what her mind was telling her.**
This **wasn't possible.**
This **couldn't be happening.**
But the **Other Ellie was watching her**, waiting, studying her like she had been expecting this moment.
Had been **waiting for her to understand.**
The **Walkman clicked**, the tape **reaching its final message.**
Margaret's voice **broke through the static**, her tone different now—urgent, almost pleading.
"If you've come this far, you already know the truth."
Ellie **clutched the Walkman**, her throat tightening.
The **Other Ellie took another step forward.**
Ellie **held up the poker instinctively.**
"But you don't understand it yet," the Other Ellie murmured.
The words **sent ice through Ellie's veins.**
The tape **crackled.**
Ellie swallowed, her throat **bone-dry.**
"**What is this?**" she whispered, barely recognizing her own voice. "**Who are you?**"
The **Other Ellie studied her**, something dark flickering behind her **too-familiar eyes.**
"I told you," she murmured. "**I'm you.**"
Ellie **shook her head violently.**
"That's not possible."
"Isn't it?"
The **cabin felt smaller**, the air **too thick**, pressing in from all sides.
Margaret's voice **kept going, unraveling like an old memory.**

"I had two daughters."

Ellie's **lungs ached.**

"One was taken."

The **Other Ellie's lips curled at the edges.**

"One was left behind."

Ellie **stumbled,** her body **flooded with something she couldn't name.**

Her head **spun,** her fingers **digging into the poker for grounding.**

No. No, **this couldn't be happening.**

"And one of you…"

The **Other Ellie smiled.**

It was **a small smile.**

Almost sad.

But there was something else in it.

Something **Ellie didn't recognize.**

The tape **crackled with static.**

And then Margaret's **final words came through, clear as day—**

"…doesn't belong."

The Truth That Shouldn't Exist

Ellie's **knees nearly buckled.**

Her body suddenly felt **wrong, like it wasn't really hers.**

Like she **wasn't really here.**

The **Other Ellie** just **watched.**

Waiting.

Letting her **figure it out on her own.**

Ellie's mind **raced.**

One was taken. One was left behind. One doesn't belong.

Had she been the **replacement for Astrid?**

Had **Astrid somehow become her?**

Or—

Her **breath caught.**

What if Astrid had **never left at all?**

What if she had simply been **rewritten?**
Ellie's **fingers curled into her palms.**
"That's not possible."
The **Other Ellie sighed.**
"You keep saying that."
The tape **clicked off.**
Silence.
Outside, the **wind howled through the trees.**
Ellie's **vision blurred.**
She had **to move.**
Had to **get out.**
But the **Other Ellie took another step forward.**
Her **eyes darkened.**
"You should have left it alone."
Ellie **tightened her grip on the poker.**
"**What are you?**" she whispered.
The **Other Ellie tilted her head.**
Then, in a voice **that echoed like a memory, she said—**
"Ellie... it's you."

Static. **Darkness.**

The **air crackled, pulling inward, warping like the cabin itself was unraveling.**

The **Other Ellie lunged.**

Ellie **swung the poker.**

A sharp **CRACK** split the air—metal **colliding with flesh.**

The **Other Ellie staggered back—but she didn't scream.**

She didn't even **flinch.**

She just... **smiled.**

And then—

The **lights flickered.**

The **air pulled tight.**

The **Walkman—long dead—suddenly played one last, garbled whisper.**

Margaret's **final message.**
"**...It's already started.**"
Ellie's **vision blurred.**
The world **fractured.**
And then—
Everything **went black.**

PROLOGUE - THE UNDEVELOPED PAST

(*Book 2: Develop & Destroy*)

The **camera felt heavy** in Ash's hands.

She turned it over, her fingers brushing against the worn leather casing. The thrift store owner had told her it was **a rare find**, an old **Canon AE-1** from the '80s.

But that wasn't what caught her attention.

It was the **film roll inside.**

A **completely undeveloped roll of Kodak film**, still wound tight inside the camera.

She stared at it, a strange unease creeping up her spine.

Because when she had held the camera for the first time, something had **flashed in her mind.**

A cabin.

A woman's voice, distorted and fading.

And the feeling that she had **been here before.**

Even though she had never stepped foot in Montana in her life.

Ash swallowed hard and shoved the camera into her bag. She would **develop the film tomorrow**.

Maybe it was nothing.

Maybe it was just **old, forgotten images**—snapshots from a stranger's life.

Or maybe—

Maybe it was something else.

Something she **wasn't supposed to find.**

And when she saw the pictures for the first time, **she would realize the truth.**

She wasn't just looking at **memories from the past.**

She was looking at **herself.**

And she had no idea **how that was possible.**

www.ingramcontent.com/pod-product-compliance
Lightning Source LLC
LaVergne TN
LVHW020444080526
838202LV00055B/5333